MY PAPA IS IMPORTANT !

BY: MISS. NATASHA

My Papa Is Important!

My Papa is Important!

My Papa is Important!

My Papa reads to me and tells me the best stories

My Papa helps me understand my homework

Papa helps me get ready for school

My
Papa takes good care of himself

My
Papa is
Important

My
Papa is
Important

My
Papa is
Important

My
Papa is
Important

My
Papa is
Important

My
Papa is
Important

My
Papa is
Important

My Papa gives me hugs and takes me for bike rides

My Papa is important

My Papa is strong like a bear and tall as a giraffe

My Papa makes me dinner
and gives me paint to
paint pictures all day long

My Papa gives me rides on his back

My Papa showed me how to make yummy cookies

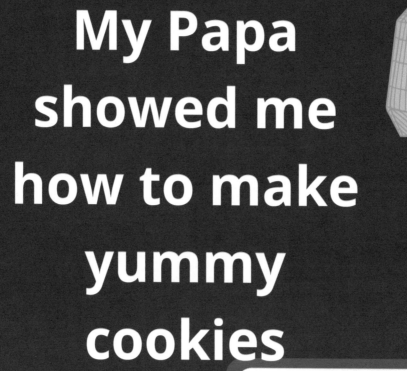

My Papa is Important!
He gives me courage and
LOVE

My Papa is Important!

He calls to check up on me from work and...

He keeps me safe from scary things

My Papa takes me on long walks and hikes

We paint rocks we found from our walk

Please oh please remember why Papa's are important !

My Papa is very much important to me!

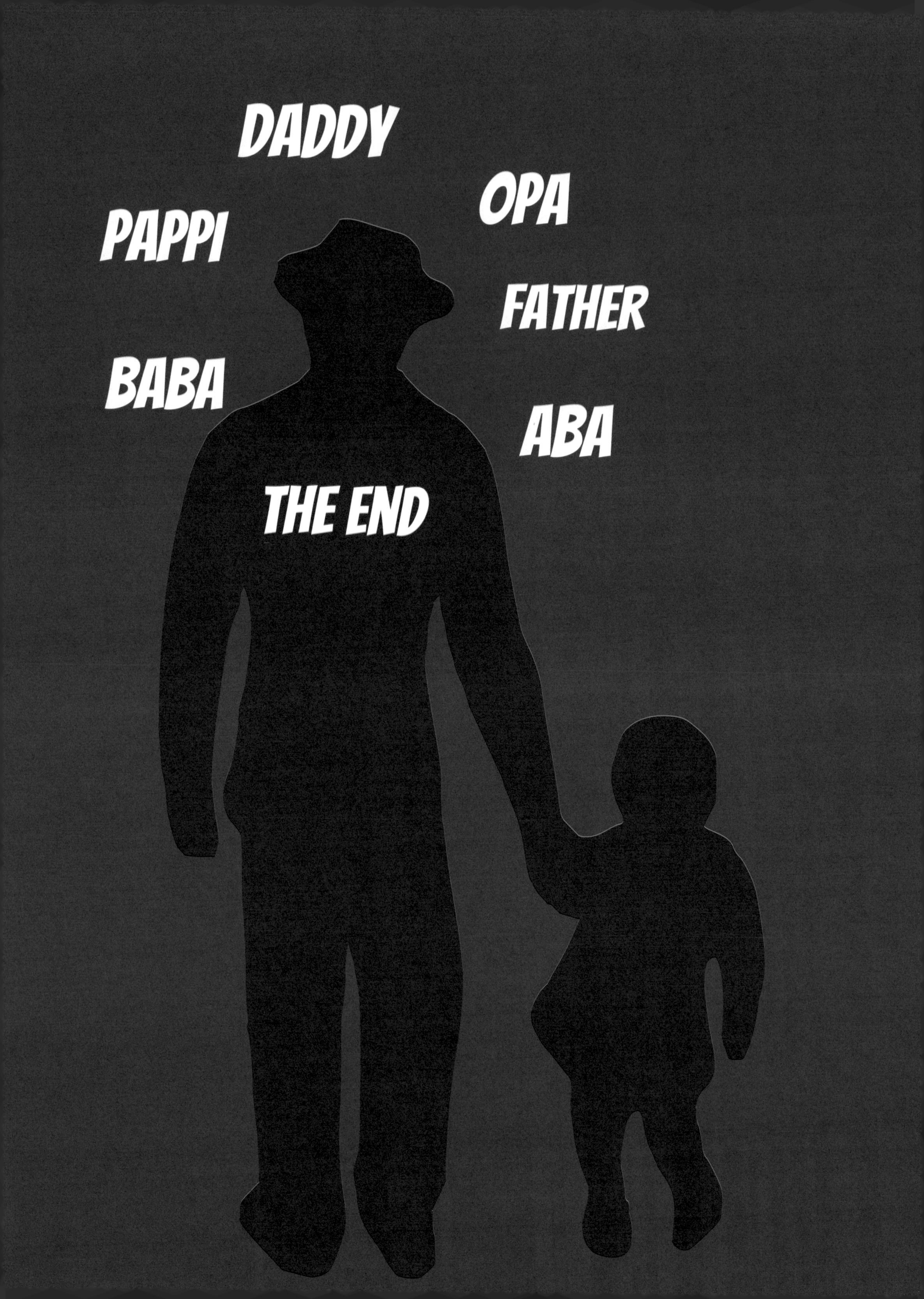
DADDY
PAPPI
OPA
FATHER
BABA
ABA
THE END

MY PAPA IS IMPORTANT!

BY: MISS. NATASHA

Made in the USA
Columbia, SC
29 June 2024

37819484R00015